WAGING WAR
—————*for your*—————
MARRIAGE

KELDRIC & KATRINA EMERY

CONTENTS

DEDICATION

This labor of love is dedicated to our children (Irvin, Omar, and Matthew). It is our prayer that this work will help you during the highs and lows of your marriages. It is our prayer that GOD will bless your marriages and remind you of GOD's faithfulness during your marriages.

We also would like to dedicate this work to the great examples who have influenced and encouraged us throughout the years. Our parents, uncles, aunts, cousins, etc.

We would lastly like to dedicate this work to our family and loved ones whose memories we hold dear to our hearts. (Ervin "Ray" Patterson, Snoweana E. Emery, Edward "Cabbage," Francis, Catherine, Keila, Simon, Irene "Barbara," Jonathan, Bennie and to all those not mentioned.

INTRODUCTION
Why are we writing this book?

It's December 25, 2020, and I am relaxing with my family. I received a call from a friend. My first thoughts are that my friend is calling me to wish me a Merry Christmas since we cannot physically be together due to the COVID-19 pandemic. My friend then goes on in a panicked tone asking if I can marry a couple. I am a licensed minister of the gospel, but I have yet to marry anyone. My wife and I have performed premarital counseling but have yet to perform the ceremony.

I answer my friend on the phone with much hesitation. 'Yes, I can marry the couple, when is the wedding in 2021?'

My friend hesitantly says 'tomorrow.'

I am just silent. There are a multitude of things flowing through my mind. How can I perform a ceremony for someone that I have never met? Should I do this?

My friend interrupted my thoughts with "The minister who was scheduled to do it has the coronavirus".

I then told my friend to call one of the other ministers on our church staff as I just don't think it is good for me to marry someone that I have never met.

After prayerful consideration and a discussion with a mentor. I decided to perform the wedding ceremony. The next day Katrina (my co-author) and I are on our way to perform our first wedding. We are full of questions and what if's, not really sure of anything but the fact that we will be there. Our mindset is that we are willing to help this couple, and actually proud that whoever they are, they are choosing to honor GOD through marriage. We arrive at the location and meet this couple who are just delightful. I think we were expecting a large wedding with a ton of people, but to our surprise, there were seven people in attendance, *total*. Despite our expectations, there was such an atmosphere of love between these two people. So, despite the number of attendees and the lack of pomp and circumstance most weddings have, Katrina and I found ourselves reminded of what it is like to be young and in love. The couple could barely read their own vows without tears. We were also reminded of what our love was like in the first years of marriage. It was truly touching.

Later the next day Katrina and I were on a zoom call with a few couples/friends. We normally get together this time of year, so we had to settle for a zoom call just to stay in touch. I asked about one of the couples that is normally in attendance and found that they are separated. My wife and I were filled with sorrow and confusion. How could this couple even consider divorce? We remember their wedding, their children, their love for each other. What happened?

We then began to realize that something happens between what we experienced from the wedding Saturday to our friends considering divorce on Sunday. What did we do to make our marriage last for 20 years? How do you wage war for your marriage and make it last? We don't claim to know everything. We do think GOD has given us a unique perspective that has allowed us to be married for 20 years and still love/like each other. Keep reading to find out how we wage war for our marriage

CHAPTER 1

Purpose of Marriage

What is the Purpose of Marriage?

arriage is GOD's idea. Therefore I think we need to look in GOD's word to find its purpose. You can see marriage in the first chapters of Genesis and two of the three purposes of marriage. I believe the other purpose can be found in Ephesians 5. The biblical purposes for marriage are as follows:

1. Procreation
2. Companionship
3. Illustration (Ephesians 5)

Procreation can be found in Genesis 1:28, *KJV*, "And God blessed them, and God said unto them, Be fruitful, and multiply, and replenish the earth, and subdue it: and have dominion over the fish of the sea, and over the fowl of the air, and over every living thing that moveth upon the earth."

Procreation is not just about making babies. It is a command to keep multiplying and expanding GOD's Kingdom. You can see the concept in the scriptures when referencing the children of Israel and how GOD wanted the children of Israel to teach their children his ways. According to Deuteronomy 11:18-21, *New International Version*, we should, "Fix these words of mine in your hearts and minds; tie them as symbols on your hands and bind them on your foreheads. Teach them to your children, talking about them when you sit at home and when you walk along the road, when you lie down and when you get up. Write them on the doorframes of your houses and on your gates, so that your days and the days of your children may be many in the land the Lord swore to give your ancestors, as many as the days that the heavens are above the earth."

The act of marriage is not only filling the earth but doing so while expanding the Kingdom of GOD. When we have parents, who want to be Christ like, they raise children with that same mind set. Society benefits from a ton of believers who want to live Christ.

Companionship can be found in Genesis 2:18, The Lord God said, "It is not good for the man to be alone. I will make a helper suitable for him."

There is something about man being alone that is not good. God thinks that companionship is so important that he created a helper suited for Adam. Marriage is

God's gift to mankind because we should not be alone. GOD created and designed us for relationships with HIM and with each other. We all have an embedded desire for relationship and community. GOD has created us this way and marriage is one of the solutions to the relationship and community that we need. GOD does not want us to be alone.

The final purpose of marriage I will discuss is illustration. People should look at marriage and see how Christ loves and cares for his church. An example can be seen in Ephesians 5. We are the unspoken example of Christ's love. When our marriages are long lasting and full of commitment, love, and forgiveness, we exemplify Jesus Christ and how He loves us. Marriage is one of the greatest witnessing tools in existence today. Healthy marriages build healthy families. Healthy marriages build healthy communities, churches, and even nations. If we love our spouses like Christ loves the church, we are fulfilling Christ's commandment.

Let's read further to keep our marriages and find out how we can love our spouses the way Christ loved the church. Let's wage war for our marriages.

Discussion Questions:

1. Do you find that marriage is still relevant to those who are in your age group?Why/Why not?

2. Do you see your marriage as a witnessing tool? Why or why Not?

3. After reading this chapter, do you feel procreation is just the act of multiplying people or multiplying GOD's kingdom? Or Both

CHAPTER 2

Wage War with Weapon of Respect (Man's Need)

As a child, I loved late-night shows, such as Johnny Carson, David Letterman, Arsenio Hall, and the list goes on. I would sneak out of my bedroom to watch the front room's TV and laugh as quietly as I possibly could to avoid getting caught. One of the guests I would frequently see on Johnny Carson and David Letterman would be Rodney Dangerfield. His classic joke was, "No Respect." Rodney would go on to talk about how his wife and everyone else in the world showed him no respect. Rodney Dangerfield makes light of one of the main problems men feel every day. Sometimes men feel no respect in their jobs, no respect in society, and worst of all no respect in their marriage. Whether we know it or not, respect is an essential need for men. This need is so great that GOD would have Paul write this statement in Ephesians 5:33, "However, each one of you also must love his wife as he loves himself, and the wife must respect her husband."

Paul, through God's wisdom, shows the keys of the marital needs of the husband and wife. A wife needs love and a husband needs respect. I, Keldric, will discuss this portion of respect from a man's perspective to the wives.

(So, ladies, listen up. Katrina will discuss love, the wife's need, in the next chapter). In the passage above Paul tells the wives to respect their husbands. When we look the word up in the Greek, it means to hold in high regard or to reverence. Please understand your husband should not be respected on the same level with GOD, but nonetheless He should have a place of reverence or respect in your life. So, what does respect look like from a wife to a husband? After researching more, I have come up with four ways I believe a wife can begin to show her husband respect.

1. Decision making – The first area concerns decision making. A wife should allow her husband to make decisions in the appropriate areas. I believe sometimes wives can make decisions without consulting their husband and can make a husband feel disrespected. It makes the husband feel as if he is not capable or sufficient. This area can be silent, but a large amount of resentment can build up over the years. Some husbands will keep taking it and not say anything until suddenly they just blow up or react in a way that is outside of

their character. It is a result of the husband not being able to fulfill his role as the leader of the home and family. Simply put, don't just tell the man what to do. Even if you know what he is going to say or do, don't assume the responsibility of what he is going to do. It is important the husband feels confident in making decisions that affect his family in a positive manner. Although Husbands will have to grow in this area, continue to encourage them so that they don't quit. They get tired of fighting with everyone. Fight on the job, fight with the children, fight in society to be respected by the time the man gets to the wife and she wants to fight again, he has just had enough. He needs to know that you trust him enough to allow him to make decisions.

2. Conversation - The second area concerns your speech toward your husband. Speak well of your husband. When a wife speaks of a husband in a derogatory manner it hurts, and it is disrespectful. The husband may even laugh and not say anything, but no man wants to pledge his life to

love someone, yet they speak better of strangers than their husband. Wives, I know your husband has bad habits and makes a lot of mistakes, but the hard truth of the matter is you picked him. You said, "yes," when he asked. You walked down the aisle, and you stood before the preacher or justice of the peace. It will do your husband all the good in the world if you just replace your criticism with an uplifting word. I can tell you from a man's perspective, sometimes by the time I have gone through my day from work, to society, to friends, and maybe church, I have been criticized and corrected maybe 10 times in one day. It is hard to come home to another level of demeaning and critical talk. It can almost be too much to bear. Speak life over your husband. It doesn't mean everything you say must be positive. Try to make sure you speak more uplifting words, words that make a man feel respected.

3. Position - The third area concerns the position your husband holds. In essence husbands and wives are the same. In value, husbands and

wives are the same. In position, we are different. Ephesians 5:23-31 is a discourse where Paul taught on the positions of husbands and wives. Paul says that the relationship between a husband and wife should mirror that of Jesus Christ and the Church. Just as the Church submits to Christ, The wife should submit to the husband. The position is not about value but about the structure and order that GOD has in place. The husband holds a different position than the wife. I think it would be very helpful if a wife remembers her husband's position is different from her own position. When the wife holds the position of another man at a greater level than her husband, this can cause the husband to feel disrespected. The husband wants to know that his opinion and thoughts regarding a matter are respected by his wife. The husband wants to know that even if the world believes he is worthless, his wife believes in him and sees him in the best light.

4. Showing your husband you need him - I understand that some of you ladies read this portion and say "you don't need anyone". You can do it

all alone. I understand what you are saying, and I respect your position. Ladies, please give my thoughts some consideration. I think one of the most hurtful things you can say to a man who loves you is, "I don't need you, and I don't need your help." It bruises a man's ego and makes him feel unappreciated when you respond in such a way. He, too, wants to feel he is important and valued in the relationship.

Here is a litmus test to try. I believe it will prove my point.

Litmus test: Find a jar in the kitchen or something you might normally not need your husband's help to achieve. I want you to ask him for his help but say it using the following words.

"Hey baby, I need you, could you please help me with _____?"

Watch as this man bends over backwards to accomplish whatever task you ask him to do. You also might catch a smile after he finishes the work.

These simple reminders are just a few ways you can show respect to your husband. I am sure there are other ways I did not mention. Ladies, please try these suggestions. I believe you will see a response of love from your husband when he feels respected by you.

Discussion Questions:

1. How can you show your husband respect through your decision making?

2. Do you think words of encouragement help or hinder the level of respect a man feels? Why?

3. Name a time when you have tried the Litmus Test and what was the outcome?

CHAPTER 3

Love Your Wife

L ove… Just a simple four letter word but women are wired and designed for it. We are designed to give and receive it. As little girls, our first bedtime stories read to us, books we independently choose to read, songs we sing, poems we recite, etc… for the most part, all these things revolve around love. They encompass either the acceptance, pursuit, and/ or desire of love. We want the happily ever after, to hear and remember the date, time and place when our significant other uttered the words, 'I love you,' for the first time.

We could be categorized as being obsessed with love and how the world presents love to us. However, we don't really get one of the realities of the concept of love until we become a *wife.* Marital love lives on many levels, but I would like to delve into the communication and partnership aspects of love.

In Ephesians 5:25-27, Paul is crystal clear concerning the tender way in which husbands are to genuinely love their wives:

> *Husbands love your wives just as Christ*
> *loved the church and gave himself up for her*

to make her holy, cleansing her by the wash-
ing with water through the word, and to
present her to himself as a radiant church,
without stain or wrinkle or any other blem-
ish but holy and blameless. (NIV)

Marriage is a heavy and serious position to be in. It is nothing to be entered into lightly. As a man, you have to grapple with loving someone as Christ loved the church, keeping in mind Christ died for the church. Again, it's why the decision to be married should not be entered into haphazardly. Much prayer and thought should go into the decision. In marriage, husbands should be willing to sacrifice everything for their wives. That's the example Christ set before us. Husbands should care for their wives as they do themselves, which again is the example Christ set before us with His care for His church. The weight of the responsibility can be overwhelming, but if loved in this way, women are intricately, precisely programmed and wired to reciprocate this love perfectly back to their husbands. It's truly a beautiful dance. It is smooth and effortless, especially if you plan to practice the steps to be in sync. Therefore, men, loving your wife should involve clear, effective communication, time, and support.

There are certain movies I can watch over and over again. One that comes to the mind is *A Thin Line Between Love and Hate*. The movie stars Lynn Whitfield and Martin Lawrence. In the movie, Martin, who plays the character, Marcus, prides himself on being a 'player,' a 'ladies man.' However, he becomes smitten by the mere appearance of Lynn, who plays the character, Brandi, and goes completely out of his way to 'get with her.' He pursues her and even gets out of his normal character and utters the words, 'I love you,' to her and his life is forever changed. See, they were just words to Marcus, but to Brandi, they meant everything.

Words encompass the sentences that make up conversations. Those very conversations are key in every marriage. Communication is where most couples either sink or swim. The ability to be open, honest, and transparent with your partner is very liberating. Most women are more communicative than men. We're the ones willing to share how we're feeling and share all our emotions.

Most men, not all, aren't big talkers, and that's where some relationships suffer. Learning how to communicate is essential.

Women require effective communication, and how you communicate can also show a form of respect. The way you love her can also be reflective of how you respect her position in your life. Some women require time, communication, gifts or any number of things collectively or separately, but ultimately, loving her will be evident in how you treat her. Women require 'studying.' Just like you study or studied in school. If you desire a positive, long lasting result, some intentional time should be spent in dissecting the love of your life.

For instance, some men have gone out of their way to surprise their spouse with an elaborate gift, let's say a vehicle. Then, when he pulls up with the vehicle, he doesn't get the response he expected. Why? His wife feels love when her husband communicates with her, and the type of surprise she received is not what she would deem considerate. It's perceived as almost disrespectful of her position in the marriage, even if a new vehicle is needed.

She's left feeling like an afterthought due to the decision being made without her input. Although she may love receiving gifts, a gift of this magnitude, without communication, can come across as disrespectful. In some cases, it can leave the wife feeling unloved, despite the intention.

> I am sure that the average marriage person would agree that marriages can feel like they are stuck on a merry go round from time to time. The keys to stopping the forever spinning are intentional communication and mutual respect. Intentional communication is transparent and honest, heart to heart. We're listening to comprehend on the heart level and not for a rebuttal. Even when the world is spinning around you, as a couple, the two of you take the time to find quiet time to sit and talk, listen, and return to the core of your love.

We can all get busy with keeping busy, the hustle and bustle of life. Throw in kids, taking care of the house and possibly working, it all can be overwhelming. Our marriages should be our safe havens. They can be if we learn how to truly fight for our marriage. The enemy will use any device he can to infiltrate any weak areas. In this case, you have to have tactical planning. Vow to each other to never go to bed angry, if you can help it. My husband knows I don't like to discuss money issues before we go to bed. Even though I deal with checks and balances all day, before bed, I don't want to know how much needs to be sent or what needs to be bought. I've communicated it clearly, and he loves me enough to respect my request.

> As mentioned before, marriage can be compared to dancing. Men always lead, and women keep the tempo, making sure the pace of movement is comfortable for the dance to last. Learning this 'marriage' dance requires time. The quality of time is different from season to season. The earliest season is spent learning likes and dislikes, negotiables and nonnegotiables. As time passes, each person learns more and

more about the other. You have to see each other as partners, partners who actually need each other to make a move.

Have you ever seen two people on a dance floor and each person looks as if they're individually dancing to a different song? The image can be either excruciating or hilarious, but it can also be dangerous. When two people have effectively communicated, respected each other's position, and considered the other a true partner, the 'dance,' or marriage just flows. The couple eases from one move to the next, taking subtle cues, gentle touches, quick glances to make their collective movement work seamlessly.

I'm sure different relationship experts or many others would say showing A woman love, or loving a woman properly, requires more than communication, respect, and partnership. Yet I truly believe when a woman receives those three things, all other things fall into place.

Discussion Questions:

1. How do you see marriage as a dance?

2. How important is it for each person to play their part to make the dance flow smoothly?

3. What are three things a woman needs to receive before all other things fall into place?

4. What can you, as a man, do to communicate better in your marriage?

CHAPTER 4

MYOB – Mind Your Own Business

Excuse me as I pull up my soap box for a moment and stand on it. As I write this statement, social media is filled with the faults and fragility of men and women who have said one thing publicly and lived a different thing privately. The truth is we all need GOD's grace. We are not perfect people. Jesus is the only perfect person who lived, died, and rose again for our redemption. Personally, I have found I can strengthen my marriage by minding my own business.

When the Apostle Paul wrote to the church at Thessalonica, he said, "... and to make it your ambition to lead a quiet life: You should mind your own business and work with your hands, just as we told you" (1 Thessalonians 4:11, *NIV*). You don't have to be a theologian to understand, "... lead a quiet life" and "... mind your own business" (1 Thessalonians 4:11, *NIV*). Your marriage can benefit from these statements. We are so concerned about reality tv and marriages of the people who are in the public eye, we forgot to pay attention to our spouses. When I concentrated on being present in my relationship with my wife I found there was so much work I needed to do. I don't have time to consider anyone else's marriage. With the rise of social media and all the instant information that is easily accessible, we often forget to do the simple task of minding our own business.

How can we mind our own business in our marriage?

1. Don't compare yourself or your spouse to someone else.
2. Study your spouse.
3. Work on the things you find after you study your spouse.
4. Fix things you can control, such as...

   a. Your attitude
   b. Your relationship with your children
   c. Your car (or lack thereof)
   d. Your house (or lack thereof)
   e. Your clothes
   f. Your dishes
   g. Your grass

Hopefully, you get the point. We can all learn a lesson from the little girl in the viral video filmed in the back seat of her parent's car. "Worry about yourself." The grammar is not the best, but it can be interpreted as a Biblical stance on minding your own business.

Discussion Questions:

1. What are ways minding our own business can help our marriage?

2. How can you study your spouse?

3. Is it important to not compare yourself or your spouse to someone else?

CHAPTER

Fight with a Financial Plan

This chapter will not be the most popular, yet I believe it can be just as helpful. It will not be a chapter where I will tell you exactly how to spend your money or ask you to commit to my financial advice. I will recommend that you have a plan you and your spouse can agree upon. Statistics from the 2012 study on <u>Hawkins, Willoughby, and Doherty</u> found 40% of marriages end in divorce due to the way the couple's money is handled. I believe it is because two different people have two different ideas on how money should be handled, and they are not on the same page. I think it is vitally important both husband and wife be on one accord concerning money and spiritual matters. If we both have decided tithing is something we are going to do then it should not be a point of contention. If we both have decided we are going to save money for an anniversary trip, my eating a sandwich instead of a fancy meal now has a purpose. The larger question is how can we get on the same page?

Here are a few suggestions we have found that have aided us:

Tip 1 - Honor GOD first in your finances (whether you believe in tithing or not). Regardless of your stance on tithes, you should at least understand that if you refuse to honor GOD by giving to your local church you must ask yourself, "Is GOD my GOD, or is Money my god?" Please understand it is only by GOD's grace that you have your job or the creative ability to provide for yourself. Find a way to honor GOD, and HE (GOD) will take care of you. I am a living witness.

Tip 2 - *Sit down together, and make a financial plan.* Take a 30-day calendar, and write out who pays what bills and the timeframe the bills should be paid. It will cause less strife in the home if you agree on who pays what bills. It will also allow you to discuss if any changes need to be made.

Tip 3 - *Create an agreed upon spending limit that requires mutual agreement.* For example, you might say we should not spend more than 500 dollars without both of us agreeing to it. This arrangement brings clarity and balance to your financial situation. If you are a free spender and your spouse is a more frugal person, when you get ready to make a purchase your spouse will balance you out. An example of that is one person shouldn't buy a new house or car without his or her spouse being involved in the purchase. It might sound very simple, but something of this nature can save you from resentment and bitterness.

Tip 4 - *Prove yourself to be a trustworthy spouse.* Do what you say you are going to do. Keep your family in mind first. Don't go spend $1,000 on a weekend trip, while your bills are unpaid. Sometimes, as the old folks say, you just have to go sit down somewhere until you can do better. Be trustworthy, and stick to your financial plan.

Tip 5 - *Include finances to enjoy life in your plan.* Create memories, take vacations, travel, take the family to the beach, and just plain relax. We sometimes get so caught up in trying to make everything perfect we don't enjoy life. Life is so short. GOD wants us to enjoy our families and our life. Don't be so frugal you cannot take your wife out to eat. Don't be so frugal you cannot buy your husband those new headphones he wanted for Father's Day. Life is for the living, so *live*. Take that anniversary trip! Take the kids to Disney World! Live life! Don't work 24/7, 365 and never take a day off. Just remember to have balance, and allow the Holy Spirit to lead you in every endeavor of your financial plan.

Discussion Questions:

1. What financial advice do you believe was ill-advised or in error?

2. What do you think about the agreed upon spending limit? Is it liberating or restricting?

3. What does a financial plan look like for you?

CHAPTER 6

Wage War with Weapon of Forgiveness

In Luke 17:1, Jesus is warning the disciples, "offenses will come." It doesn't matter who you are, single or married, young or old, at some point someone will offend you. You can be assured if Jesus says offenses will come, your spouse will offend you. He or she will offend you with intention or without. Nevertheless, offense will happen. I think the larger question is how do you get past the offense. How do you forgive someone for disrespectful behavior? How do you forgive someone for demeaning or degrading comments? How do you forgive someone who knew doing a particular thing would hurt your heart? How do you forgive someone who has betrayed your trust and been unfaithful? How do you forgive in your marriage?

Before we discuss what forgiveness consists of, I believe I need to elaborate on what forgiveness is not. Here is a list (not exhaustive) of what forgiveness is not:

1. Forgiveness does not mean reconciliation or restoring. Forgiveness does not mean you must restore the relationship. Forgiveness is a necessity.

Reconciliation is not always possible. In the case of violence or abuse, safety should be your priority.

2. Forgiveness is not returning to the way things were before the incident. There should be steps made toward trust and rebuilding. It also depends on the severity of the infraction. If someone steps on your shoe, things can go back to the way they were pretty swiftly. If someone steals your retirement and commits adultery with a different person, there should be a timeframe for which restoration and reconciliation happen. You should forgive the person as soon as possible. You probably should *not* trust the person.

3. Forgiveness is not ignoring or forgetting. Forgiveness is not pretending nothing ever happened or that you don't have to address the issue at hand. I believe in Christian counseling, and I think it is helpful and necessary. When someone acts as if nothing ever happened, I believe

it causes resentment. Resentment can turn into bitterness. Bitterness can and will turn into hate if it is not addressed. As much as it hurts we need to deal with the issue.

4. Forgiveness is not tolerating or allowing further abuse. If you are a victim of abuse, please seek refuge and safety. Forgiveness does not require you to allow someone to abuse you or harm you. GOD loves you, and it is my prayer you love yourself and seek help. (Domestic Abuse National Hotline Number: 1.800.799.7233)

5. Forgiveness is not escaping consequences or justice. Just because you forgive someone does not mean they should not be held responsible for their indiscretion. For example, Pope John Paul II was crossing St. Peters Square in Vatican City (1981) when an attempt was made to assassinate him. Pope John Paul II was shot twice by Mehmet Ali Ağca. Despite severe blood loss, Pope John Paul survived, and asked for all Catholics to pray for Ağca, whom he had 'sincerely forgiven.' In 1983,

Pope John Paul II visited Agca. They had a private conversation and emerged as friends. The pope stayed in touch with Ağca's family during his incarceration, and in the year 2000 requested he be pardoned. Pope John Paul held Agca accountable for his behavior, yet he forgave him. People should be held responsible for their actions, yet we can forgive them and not hold hatred in our hearts toward them.

6. Forgiveness does not mean condoning or excusing the behavior or the offensive act. We can forgive people yet understand the behavior is not acceptable. Forgiveness does not mean we agree with what people do or agree with their behavior. We understand the behavior is wrong, yet we forgive them because GOD has forgiven us.

7. Forgiveness does not leave you feeling all good inside. (Forgiveness is not based on your emotions). When you decide to forgive someone, your mind and emotions might not always agree with you. We will talk about what forgiveness is in the next

section, but be assured you don't have to always obey your feelings. Your feelings are not the most reliable source. Your feelings will say, 'Don't go to work.' Hopefully, you are mature enough to understand you need your job and having a job in this economy is a blessing. Hopefully, you go to work anyway and realize feelings change. Feelings follow action. Referring back to the work example, have you ever not felt like going to work, but by the end of the day, you are happy you went? In the same vein, you must push past how you feel, and do what GOD has commanded you to do and forgive.

What is forgiveness and how do you forgive?

Psychology Today defines forgives in the following way:

"Forgiveness is, in part, a willingness to drop the narrative on a particular injustice, to stop telling ourselves over and over again the story of what happened, what [the] other person did, how we were injured, and all the rest of the upsetting things we remind ourselves in relation to this unforgivable-ness. It's a decision to let the past be what it was, to leave it as is, imperfect and not what we wish it had been. Forgiveness means we stop the shoulda, coulda, woulda been-s and relinquish the idea that we can create a different (better) past"

(https://www.psychologytoday.com/us/blog/inviting-monkey-tea/201803/what-is-forgiveness-and-how-do-you-do-it).

Peter asks Jesus how many times we should forgive someone, which I believe is a very good question. Peter then gives a suggestion, 'seven times.' During Jesus and Peter's time, most people believed in the three-strikes rule. Peter was trying to show Jesus he's a really great person, so he said seven. Jesus blows that away with a number we cannot fathom (seventy times seven).

Jesus thinks forgiveness is so essential He illustrated forgiveness with the below parable:

The Parable of the Unforgiving Servant

Then Peter came up and said to him, "Lord, how often will my brother sin against me, and I forgive him? As many as seven times?" Jesus said to him, "I do not say to you seven times but seventy-seven times. Therefore the kingdom of heaven may be compared to a king who wished to settle accounts with his servants. When he began to settle, one was brought to him who owed him ten thousand talents. And since he could not pay, his master ordered him to be sold, with his wife and children and all that he had, and payment to be made. So the servant fell on his knees, imploring him, 'Have patience with me, and I will pay you everything.' And out of pity for him, the master of that servant released him and forgave him the debt. But when that same servant went out, he found one of his fellow servants who owed him a hundred denarii, and seizing him, he began to choke him, saying, 'Pay what you owe.' So his fellow servant fell down and pleaded with him, 'Have patience with me, and I will pay you.' He refused and went and put him in prison until he could pay the debt. When his fellow servants saw what had taken place, they were greatly distressed, and they went and reported to their master all that had taken place. Then his master summoned him and said to him, 'You wicked servant! I forgave you all that debt because you pleaded with me. And should not you have had mercy on your fellow servant, as I had mercy on you?' And in anger his master delivered him to the jailers, until he should pay all his debt. So also my heavenly Father will do to every one of you, if you do not forgive your brother from your heart." (Matthew 18:21-35, *English Standard Version*)

When we consider how much we have sinned against God, we consider the large debt we owe GOD for our sins. How could we hold someone else hostage for the small amount they owe us?

Forgiveness is to release someone from the debt they owe you. In short, forgiveness means to let go of the offense someone owes you. It means you will not pay them back for what they have done. It also means you let go of negative emotions, and do not hold the person captive through your anger, resentment, hatred, etc.

How do you forgive?

By profession, I, Keldric, am an Infrastructure Engineer. I spend the majority of my day resolving technical issues, finding errors, and trying to prevent problems before they happen. My personality aids me in my job, but it has not been so helpful in my marriage. In the earlier years of our marriage, my natural knack of fault finding has hurt my wife in a number of ways and a number of times. I can remember early in our marriage our first anniversary came around, and I made it a point to go out of my way and make a big deal of it. Flowers, a big gift, dinner... the whole nine yards. After I did all of that, she got me a card that said, 'Happy Anniversary.' That's it. I was furious. I made all kinds of accusations and said all kinds of unkind words. The truth of the matter is I was hurt. I had a concept of what an anniversary should be like and that was not it. Instead of expressing what was going on, I went left and began to accuse her of the worst. I allowed my emotions to take the wheel, and I went wherever they (my emotions) drove.

We were a young couple with two young kids, with anger, resentment and unforgiveness between us. I was angry because I only got a card; she was rightfully angry because I made accusations and spoke unkindly. I later realized it was all my fault, and I needed to ask her to forgive me.

Here is how we forgive:

1. **Go to your wife/husband and discuss the offense. (Matthew 18:15-20).** Too often, we don't do the simple things, like telling the person how we feel and what has offended us. When you approach your spouse, you should go with phrases like, "When _____ happened it made/ makes me feel like_____." Please don't go to your spouse with accusations and/or a demeaning tone. Remember, tone is more than 40% of how we perceive a message. Remember to go to your spouse and not Facebook, Instagram, Twitter, etc. Going to anyone else before you go to your spouse about your offense is like setting a pile of leaves on

fire then walking away. The leaves might burn out (not causing much damage), or the leaves might burn down the entire neighborhood. Keep your offenses between the two of you. Sometimes it is acceptable to get *good* counsel. Make sure your council is wise and can keep your business safe. Be very careful about discussing your marriage with other people. If you are unsure, don't do it.

2. **Humanize the person who has wronged you. (Matthew 18:27).** When someone has wronged me, I realize I don't see the person the way I see myself. I see the person as an object of evil meant to hurt me intentionally. I don't see the person with emotions or a past or even that the offense could have happened by mistake. What I didn't explain about our anniversary story is that my wife's family was in town, and she had not seen them for months. She was also nine months pregnant with our son, and his due date was around the corner. (He was born on the ninth day of that month; our anniversary is on the first day of our son's birthday month). I later realized I was so

busy looking at my feelings I never humanized my wife and put myself in her shoes. I realized she was going through so much at the time. I would have forgotten, too, if I was in her shoes.

I am asking you to humanize your spouse. Realize your spouse makes mistakes. Your spouse has rough days. Your spouse gets frustrated. Your spouse does not intend to hurt you. Remember, your spouse is human, just like you. Remember, your spouse stood before GOD and people to commit his/her life to you. Humanize him/her.

3. **Give up (surrender) your right to get even (Matthew 18:27).** We often tell people we forgive them, but we are still trying to find a way to get even. Letting go of the drive to get even or pay them back for what they have done is a part of forgiveness. What I find helps me with this process is prayer. Praying for your spouse should be something you do every day. If you are finding it hard to let go of offenses, I suggest praying for the person as much as you can. I have found when I

pray sincerely for people GOD changes my heart toward the person. GOD will do the same for you. You can forgive your spouse or anyone else, but it takes time for the process of the decision to forgive to catch up with your heart and emotions. Forgiveness is a decision not a feeling.

4. **Wish them well (Matthew 18:27).** Don't allow negative feelings regarding an offense to determine how you view your spouse forever. In other words, don't hold the offense over your spouse's head. Don't remind your spouse of the offense every opportunity you get. It also requires prayer and maturity. You will have to learn to muzzle your mouth until your heart lines up with your decision to forgive. You will have to really wish your spouse well. You will have to speak well of them and even cast down thoughts in your mind that say otherwise (2 Corinthians 10:5). Spending time daily in prayer for your spouse will aid and change your heart. Forgiveness is a process and in order to achieve it you must wage war and go after it. Your marriage is worth it!

Discussion Questions:

1. What does it mean to forgive?

2. Do you think forgiveness is important in marriage?

3. Do you find it difficult to humanize your spouse during a time when forgiveness is necessary?

4. How can sharing your offense on social media affect your marriage?

CHAPTER

Waging War with the Weapon of a Magnifying Glass

There is a scene in the Tyler Perry movie, *Why Did I Get Married?*, where Perry's character explains the 80/20 rule. The rule illustrates how people become so focused on the 20% of what their spouse does not possess, they don't appreciate the 80% their spouse does possess. This chapter is about taking the magnifying glass off the 20% and placing it on the 80%. I have found the enemy uses an underlying mindset which has plagued marriages. The mindset is discontentment. Discontent is the underlying emotional character flaw of the 80/20 rule.

Discontent will fill your heart and thoughts without letting you know it is there. You will find thoughts like:

1. Why doesn't he/she do _____ like _____?

2. Why doesn't he/she look like _____?

3. Why won't he/she act like _____'s wife/husband?

4. We must not be meant to be together because he/she doesn't do _____?

Discontentment is a trap of the enemy and a result of it is a longing that can never be satisfied. Even if our spouses behave in the way we think they should, discontentment will find a different flaw to uncover. Our insatiable discontentment will turn to inner (thoughts) or outer (complaining, whining, fussing, nagging, sharp hurtful comments, and critical statements) spoken words that will cause us to seek outside of our relationship. The larger questions are how do we address discontentment, and how do we turn the magnifying glass from the 20% to the 80%?

In Philippians chapter 4, Paul says the famous verse we all know so intimately, "I can do all things through Christ who strengthens me" (verse 13). Preceding the verse, we see Paul saying he has been in a variety of different situations, and he has learned to be content. Paul says he has lived with plenty, and he has lived in need; he has learned how to be content. I think we all need to learn to be content. We can do all things through Christ who strengthens us, including learning to be content with our current circumstances.

Here are a few ways I think we can learn to operate in contentment:

1. Stop comparing. Don't compare yourself to any-
    one, and don't compare your spouse to anyone
    else. It is a never-ending cycle, and you will never
    be satisfied (2 Corinthians 10:12).

2. Practice gratefulness. Make it a practice to NOT
    focus on the 20% of your spouse, and thank GOD
    for the 80%. I also think it is a good idea to write
    down all of the 80% things about your spouse.
    Thank GOD for the 80%.

3. If you cannot shake the constant barrage, gently
    discuss what bothers you so much about the 20%.
    If your spouse feels like it is something they are
    not willing to even consider, it has now become
    your prayer assignment. You are not praying for
    GOD to change him or her but to change you.
    You are praying GOD helps you to see the picture
    clearly as He does. You are praying it causes such
    a great love for the 80%, the 20% will not even
    matter. Sometimes situations will come in your

life you cannot change, but GOD will use them to develop your character and make you more like Jesus. I know because HE has done it for me and to me.

4. Consider yourself. Remember, we all come from different backgrounds and circumstances. We will not all be exactly the same. Give your spouse some grace because you need grace as well.

Keep waging war using the magnifying glass of contentment.

Discussion Questions:

1. Define contentment and give an example of what it looks like in your everyday life?

2. Why is contentment important in your marriage and in life?

3. Is Paul referring to contentment in Philippians 4? Does GOD want us to be content?

CHAPTER 8

Wage War with the Weapon of Prayer

If you have made it this far in the book, I am sure you can tell we are a people of prayer. It is not that I put my faith in prayer, but my faith is in a GOD who is faithful to answer prayer. As I was preparing to write this chapter, I realized how vital prayer is to the Christian faith. In the hymn, "What a Friend We Have in Jesus," part of the song says, "O what peace we often forfeit, O what needless pain we bear, all because we do not carry everything to GOD in prayer." How true those stanzas are. We all (myself included) could stand to spend more time in prayer. I will be the first to admit, in the earlier days of my marriage, I spent more time complaining to GOD about my spouse than actually praying for her. Prayer is so powerful. As you pray for others GOD has the tendency to change your heart in the process. As we delve deeper into how prayer can help your marriage, please keep in mind Jesus told us men should always pray (Luke 18:1).

This book was born from this chapter. Let us begin... I remember my wife and I really going through a tough season in our marriage. We were not seeing eye to eye and other stressors (raising children, financial stress, etc) added to the tension of the already tough season. I remember reading this passage:

We are human, but we don't wage war as humans do. We use GOD's mighty weapons, not worldly weapons, to knock down the strongholds of human reasoning and to destroy false arguments. "We destroy every proud obstacle that keeps people from knowing God. We capture their rebellious thoughts and teach them to obey Christ" (2 Corinthians 10:3-5, *New Living Translation*).

The scripture lifted off the page, and we realize we were looking at each other as if we were the problem. We didn't realize Satan was the problem. He hates marriage, and everything that reflects GOD's glory. If you remember the first chapter of the book, you remember marriage is a reflection of how Jesus loves the church. Our marriage is a living, breathing testimony of how much Jesus loves the church. We realized we cannot wage war the way the world wages war.

As Christians, we cannot use hatred, infidelity, or criticalness to keep our marriages working. That is what the world does. We should use GOD's mighty weapons. Prayer is one of those weapons.

In the simplest terms, prayer is a conversation with GOD, where you speak to GOD and then allow GOD to speak to you. In my own spiritual walk, I spend time talking to GOD, but I am learning I need to allow GOD to speak to me through prayer. I am guilty of making prayer a complaining session. Where I just talk about what all is wrong with my life and the people who have done things to me. I realize I have been praying about people and not for people. I also realize I have spent so much time talking to GOD that I have not listened to hear if he is telling me I need to change.

With all that said, you may be wondering how you should pray for your spouse? What should you say? How do you pray when you are angry? How do you pray when you are sad? These things come to mind:

1. Be devoted. Colossians 4:2 says, "Devote yourselves to prayer with an alert mind and a thankful heart." Praying for your husband or wife should be something that you do everyday.

2. Be alert. You should be alert and intentional about the way you pray for your spouse. If you see your

spouse dealing with thoughts of despair or fear, your prayers should uphold your spouse in that area. You should pray things like, "The joy of the Lord is my spouse's strength," or "God has not given my spouse the spirit of fear but of power and love and a sound mind." Be alert and specific.

3. Be grateful. Thank GOD for all HE has done and is doing for you and your spouse. Thank GOD for your spouse. Thank GOD for the trials HE has brought you through. Thank GOD for His purpose being fulfilled in your marriage and in both of your lives. Thank GOD for making your spouse more like Christ, despite what you see. Keep being grateful for all GOD has done.

If after reading those points, you are still unsure what to say or how to pray, here are examples:

This prayer is for wives:

Father, I come to you with a heart of thanksgiving for all you have done and all you are doing for me and my marriage. I thank you, Father, that you help my marriage be an example of how Christ loves the church. I thank you for your protection and provision thus far in my marriage.

Now, Father, I ask you to cleanse my heart from anything that does not please you, any sins of omission or commission. Please cleanse me through the Blood of Jesus. Father, please cleanse me of any negative feelings or emotions toward my spouse that are not like you. Help me to forgive. I know you forgave me first, for it was your SON Jesus' sacrifice that allows me to be called righteous. I accept His finished work and the gift of salvation. I know I can never be righteous without Jesus' sacrifice on the cross.

Now, Father, I come to you on behalf of my marriage and my spouse. I ask you to cover, (husband or wife's name goes here). I pray the angels of the Lord encamp around him/her keeping him/her during the day. I pray your Holy Spirit would lead and guide him/her through every step of the day and every decision made.

I pray your Holy Spirit will give my husband the wisdom to lead us in a way that pleases you. I pray you strengthen my husband in difficult times and give him peace that passes all understanding. I pray if/when he gets off track, your Holy Spirit will lead him back to a place that pleases your heart. I pray you give my husband a heart of love for me and our entire family; make him a man who wants to please you the most. Heal my husband's body and liberate his mind from the lies of the enemy.

This prayer is for husbands:

Father, I come to you with a heart of thanksgiving for all you have done and all you are doing for me and my marriage. I thank you, Father, that you help my marriage be an example of how Christ loves the church. I thank you for your protection and provision thus far in my marriage.

Now, Father, I ask you to cleanse my heart from anything that does not please you, any sins of omission or commission. Please cleanse me through the Blood of Jesus. Father, please cleanse me of any negative feelings or emotions toward my spouse that are not like you. Help me to forgive. I know you forgave me first, for it was your SON Jesus' sacrifice that allows me to be called righteous. I accept His finished work and the gift of salvation. I know I can never be righteous without Jesus' sacrifice on the cross.

Now, Father, I come to you on behalf of my marriage and my spouse. I ask you to cover, (husband or wife's name goes here). I pray the angels of the Lord encamp around him/her keeping him/her during the day. I pray your Holy Spirit would lead and guide him/her through every step of the day and every decision made.

I pray your Holy Spirit will give my wife patience and discernment as I try to lead us in a way that pleases you. Help me, Father, to be attentive to my wife when you speak through her to me. Help me to hear your voice, Father, as she gives the insight you have given to her. I pray you strengthen my wife in difficult times and give her peace that passes all understanding. I pray if/when she gets off track, your Holy Spirit will lead her back to a place that pleases your heart. I pray you give my wife a heart of love for me and our entire family; make her a woman who wants to please you the most. Heal my wife's body and liberate her mind from the lies of the enemy.

I now pray these specific scriptures over my husband or wife:

Ephesians 4:2-3: "With all humility and gentleness, with patience, bearing with one another in love, eager to maintain the unity of the Spirit in the bond of peace."

Colossians 3:14: "And over all these virtues put on love, which binds them all together in perfect unity."

Ephesians 5:25: "For husbands, this means love your wives, just as Christ loved the church. He gave up his life for her."

Genesis 2:24: "Therefore a man shall leave his father and his mother and hold fast to his wife, and they shall become one flesh."

I pray these things in the name of Jesus. Amen.

That is how you wage war in prayer for your spouse.

Discussion Questions:

1. How can you begin to pray for your spouse?

2. Do you think it is important to pray with your spouse?

3. As a practice once a month, I ask you to hold hands with your spouse and pray for them and with them. Do you think this practice will change your relationship? (Please let me know on social media what you think).

CHAPTER 9

Wage War with the Weapon of Understanding (Husbands)

Husbands Understanding Your Wife

When I was growing up, I loved music. There is a song that resonates in my mind, and it speaks to this subject. The song is "Understanding" by Xscape. The song says, "What I need from you is understanding; Can we communicate? Please hear what I say." The song reminds me we, as men, need to be intentional about understanding our wife. When I purchased this song in the '90s I am sure the writer must have thought about the following scripture:

"In the same way, you husbands, live with *your wives* in an understanding way [with great gentleness and tact, and with an intelligent regard for the marriage relationship], as with someone physically weaker, since she is a woman. Show her honor *and* respect as a fellow heir of the grace of life, so that your prayers will not be hindered *or* ineffective" (1 Peter 3:7, *Amplified Bible*).

I know there are times I am just not as understanding as I should be with my wife. I have found that when I keep these things in mind or at least as a reminder (on my phone, sticky notes, etc....) they help me to be a better husband. They help me to be more understanding of my wife's needs.

1. Security: Understand my wife's need for Security. Wives long for security. Men we need to be understanding and consider things we do to make our wives feel unsafe. Obviously, we need to take the proper measures to keep our family physically safe but sometimes we must remember that security to a wife doesn't always look like physical safety. Men, we must be steadfast with our approach to keeping our marriage and family second to GOD. This mindset followed by actions will deepen our wives sense of security in us as husbands and fathers to our children.

2. Intimacy (non-sexual affection): I have found it is an area where most men (me included) need some growth. In the crass society where nothing is left to the imagination, I still believe women secretly desire to be honored and handled with a level of gentleness. Understanding our wife's desire should cause us to remember there are

layers to intimacy. As men, we need to go the extra mile and learn when our wives need this layer of intimacy. I have found that when I understand my wife's need for this level of intimacy, it has opened other layers of intimacy in our marriage. There are an infinite amount of ways to show non-sexual affection, such as holding your wife's hand, hugging her for no reason, embracing her while watching a movie, preparing her a meal, repairing her car, etc. Understanding your wife means finding out what these things consist of and doing them. Men, this is something you will have to work toward achieving, but you will find a great reward once you work toward this goal.

3. Communication (telling her where you are): There is an entire chapter dedicated to Communication. I do believe it is important to work on communicating with our wives. Talking sometimes seems so difficult to us men. It has been said women use about 25,000 words a day; whereas man will only use about 15,000 words per day. For most men, we use those 15,000 at work. By the time we get

home, we are out of words while our wife still has 10,000 more words left after work. Men, we need to work hard to be verbal with our wives and communicate our hearts and minds. Communication is like a muscle; the more you use it, the stronger it gets. Work the muscle of communication.

4. Leadership: Husbands, this area is a need our wives will greatly appreciate. It is the need for us to take leadership yet not be domineering. It is a delicate dance we must learn to do with grace and humility. Leadership is a role we often forgo for a variety of reasons. We may feel inadequate, or we may feel like our wife just takes over when we are not doing something correctly. We don't want the tug of war. Whatever the reason, we should lead with grace and humility. Leadership does not mean you must do everything. It does mean you take the final responsibility. For example, if your wife is better at finances, you should delegate the responsibility and check with her every so often to see the status of things. I had to realize I was doing a better job at being a leader at work than

I was with my family. I would delegate at work and have status meetings. I wouldn't just leave a project undone and incomplete at work. (It would be embarrassing). Shameful to say, I realize I was not leading my family the best. I had to change and lead my family well. Husbands, lead your family well and make an intentional effort to lead your family in a direction Jesus Christ would be pleased.

Use these key points to do a better job of understanding your wife. Becoming a lifelong student of my wife, I have found I don't know everything about my wife, and the more I seek to understand and be understanding, our relationship continues to grow to a healthy place.

Discussion Questions:

1. What are some ways we can do a better job of leading our family? What does leading your family look like in practical terms?

2. How can we, as husbands, be more understanding concerning intimacy toward our wives? Do you think our wives see intimacy the same way we, husbands, see intimacy?

3. Is it important for our wives to feel secure in our marriages? What can we practically do to make our wives feel secure?

CHAPTER

10

Wage War with the Weapon of Submission: Encouragement For Wives

S ubmission is the action or fact of accepting or yielding to a superior force or to the will or authority of another person. Ephesians 5:22 (NIV) tells us, "Wives, submit yourselves to your own husbands as you do to the Lord." Biblically speaking, submission is a military word that means to bring oneself under subjection. It is not about value. We have the same value, just different positions and/or roles in Christ. Of course most, not all, women find it difficult to even discuss submission. This word aligns itself with 'obey' in most women's minds. Or the perception of submission is a form of dictatorship. For so long, the word submission has been mishandled and misused. One would think, how does submission assist in waging war for your marriage? Wouldn't being submissive put one person above the other? Or better yet, if someone is being submissive, don't they seem to be bending to the other person, never getting their way, or just plain losing in life. Honestly, someone does lose; the *enemy Satan does*, along with all the tactics and devices he uses to destroy relationships. In today's environment (culture), so much energy and time is given to assuring women of their independence, submission is never discussed at the kitchen table between women. To be clear, we can be submissive and independent simultaneously. By no means am I implying women shouldn't be independent or self-sufficient. But what I would like to shine a light on is the unspoken and neglected weapon of submission.

Of course, the Word of God gives us many scriptures on submission. There's submission of slave to master, the church to Christ, and wives to their own husbands. The order God has ordained for us to live peaceably, all of which can come with controversy today. However, in the church and in marriage, the order and exercise of submission is clear. Ephesians 5:24 states, "Now as the church submits to Christ, so also wives should submit to their husbands in everything." So the order of marriage should be that the husband is submitted to Christ, so that the wife can easily submit to her husband. Spiritually, both should be submitted to Christ, and have a personal relationship with Him. Naturally, the wife should submit to her husband to be in alignment in their marriage. It allows the marriage to be in the perfect position to win. The key to the victory is EVERYONE has to be in their position.

There's unfortunately a plethora of men who have not either seen examples or even knew they have a responsibility of submission in their lives. It's difficult to do something you've never seen or been taught. The same goes for women. There are numerous young ladies who have been raised in single-parent (mother) homes. Where the mom only submits to Christ/the church or no one. So you have several women entering into marriages not knowing how to truly submit to their husbands. On the flip side, you have young men not understanding they have to model submission to Christ, so their wives will find it easy to submit to their own husband. Again, submission is not about value but about position. It's a simple game of following the leader. God created the positions for us to live peacefully, successfully, and able to win.

If we are all honest, being submissive is either easy or extremely hard. Most couples have to learn what I will call their 'marriage rhythm.' It involves knowing when your marriage is running like a well-oiled machine and activating the true Biblical hierarchy in marriage. Let me be clear, marriage is not about someone having power over someone; that's not what we're trying to say. Sometimes you just really have to know your strong areas. Highlight them, so your marriage is successful and both people feel fulfilled and loved.

Discussion Questions:

1. What have you heard about submission (negative and/or positive)?

2. Who are some good examples of wives who balance the act of submission?

3. What does submission look like in your marriage?

CHAPTER

11

Waging War Using Communication

When I was a young man, I can remember a minister at my church by the name of Scott Baham. Scott had this saying that sticks with me till this day. He would say, "One of the biggest lies that we learned as children was, 'sticks and stones may break my bones, but words will never hurt me.'" That lie has ruined plenty of men and women in the Body of Christ, life, and marriages. When I first encountered this saying, I thought the sticks and stones thing was not too bad, but the truth is Scott was 100% right. Words hurt, and if not addressed, words can damage our mindset and even the trajectory of our life. In this chapter, we will begin by examining a few things we should keep in the forefront of our mind when communicating with our spouse.

I. **Be mindful of 'what you say.'** We all have been guilty of saying one too many words. The older I become the more I realize I need to think more and speak less. I believe as married couples we can be so careless about what we say to our spouses, not realizing how our words can hurt. I often remember the scripture that says we will be held accountable for every idle word (Matthew 12:36). That scripture humbles me and helps me to remember I need to be mindful about what I say and try not to use my words to hurt my spouse. Effective communication with my words should include patience, kindness, and truth. (Likewise, wives.....Proverbs 31:26)

II. **Be mindful of 'how you say it.'** Your tone, or how you say it, can speak volumes about what you are trying to communicate. Our tone can communicate our love, frustration, or disdain for someone with the same words that say something different. Our tone communicates 38% of what we are trying to say. If your tone says I am upset but your words say something different, we often listen to your tone and not the words. Therefore, be mindful of your tone when communicating with your spouse.

III. **Be mindful of 'how your body language communicates what you are saying.'** Our body language can communicate a large amount of what we are saying, even more than words. As a test, mute your device (i.e. TV, cell phone, tablet), and look at a video. You will not know every detail, but you will get a general idea of what is going on in the video. The body language can speak volumes. Consider a person's hands and posture when they are speaking. Are their arms folded? It could mean they are closed off to you, or they are cold. Are their hands folded? It could be a sign of nervousness. There are so many indications of what we are thinking through our body language.

Be mindful when communicating with your spouse. You may be saying one thing with your mouth, but your body language may be communicating something different. Make sure your words and body language are effectively sending the same message. I should also add that you should consider the behavior of your spouse. Your spouse may have individual quirkiness or habits in body language that may just be habitual and does not indicate your spouse is hiding something but just being him or herself.

Try these steps to improve your communication:

1. Remember we all are wrong sometimes. I believe we are so focused on getting our point across when we communicate, we don't consider the thought we could be wrong. We become so driven to prove our point, we fail to realize we can be wrong. It is really about learning to be humble and realizing even if we are right, we should remember we have been wrong in the past. We should try to keep in mind we should treat our spouse the way we want to be treated because we are wrong sometimes as well.

2. Remember listening is a part of effective communication. Notice you have two ears and one mouth. We really need to keep in mind we need to spend twice as much time listening than speaking. I am guilty of not being a good listener. One thing that has helped me is to not form a response until I hear my spouse out, and I repeat what I think my spouse has currently communicated.

Just remember to listen and hear your spouse out. It can be difficult but you can do it. Your spouse deserves to be heard out completely.

3. Remember to not be defensive. We can all be selfish. We have to check ourselves often when discussing or communicating, especially when we feel like the person speaking is attacking us. We need to remember to catch ourselves and not attack our spouses for their point of view, which is different from our own.

   It is best to try and understand the position of our spouse and how they came to his or her stance. Try to seek understanding rather than attack your spouse because intentional conflict will only escalate the conversation. Breathe, listen, and ask GOD to help you not be defensive.

4. Remember to be honest when communicating. Honesty is the roadway to gaining or regaining someone's trust. It is imperative to be honest in your marriage. Honesty and transparency help a marriage to grow stronger. It tells your spouse you

want to get to know, 'the real him/her' because you are willing to expose the 'the real you.' It shows you are willing to expose the good and bad.

Remember, marriage is a reflection of Christ's love for the church. The church has been stained by sin and shame. Christ died for the church despite the stains. We all have stains. Honesty opens the door for forgiveness and sacrificial love. It is not easy, but honesty is worth it.

5. Remember to never quit on communication. I am reminded of one scene in the movie, *Kingdom Come*, one of my and Katrina's favorites. Whoopi Goldberg's character is explaining to the pastor the type of man her husband was, so he could prepare for the eulogy. She said, "He was mean and surly." The pastor tried to rephrase her words to make the deceased man more likable. She was not having it. She repeated again, "He was mean and surly." She then went on to explain she and her husband had not spoken a kind word to each other in 22 years. My goodness! They are a vivid

example of what a couple who gave up on communicating looks like. It reminds me no matter how difficult things might be, I need to never give up on communicating with my spouse. Working towards better communication is better than not communicating at all. I surely don't want my children or my wife to remember me as silent when I should have been speaking. I don't want my children to remember me or ever consider me as mean and surly.

The Bible says a soft answer turns away wrath (Proverbs 15:1). A soft answer is still an answer. Keep working toward making communication better. Sometimes it can seem easier to just keep the peace and not say anything. Remember in scripture we are called to be peacemakers and not peacekeepers. In the Sermon on the Mount, Jesus said, "Blessed are the peacemakers (Matthew 5:9). Some of us look for peace by being peacemakers, and some of us look for peace by being a peacekeeper. A peacemaker is someone who is willing to resolve both outer and inner conflict in order to establish peace with others and within him or herself. A peacekeeper, on the other hand, wants to maintain peace by avoiding conflict. They typically give in to the tension or steer clear of disagreement to keep others happy. Peacekeepers really never keep the peace. They end up internalizing all the conflict within themselves and in some cases, blaming themselves for the conflict. I can tell you from a personal perspective, peacekeeping is hindering your communication in your relationship. Peacekeeping will cause you to be silent when you should be speaking in love. I do admit we must consider the best time to deal with the conflict, but at some point, the conflict should be addressed and discussed. I have found if I don't address the issue, it can turn into bitterness or resentment. Communication can help to make peace, but do it in love and don't bottle everything inside.

Finally, here are some questions you can use to aid in your communication. If you feel like you don't know what to say or how to describe how you feel, use the following questions during a date night, or a walk, or house work. Anything where you have each other's attention and time. You don't have to go through all of these questions at the same time. I believe it is better to discuss them one at a time.

Communication Questions:

1. What is your dream date or weekend getaway with me?

2. How can we improve our intimacy (i.e. spiritually, physically, and/or emotionally)?

3. If you had 3 wishes for your future, what would they be?

4. How am I doing as a husband or wife in general? (Use the number system from 10 (best) to 1 (needs drastic improvement)).

   Advice to the spouse asking the question: Give your spouse time to explain without interrupting.

   Advice to the spouse answering the question: Answer through the filter of love. (Don't use it as an opportunity to hurt your spouse).

5. What are you most excited or afraid about regarding our relationship during this season we currently reside?

6. If you could see two things change about me, what would they be?

7. How can I show you honor (publicly or privately)?

ABOUT THE
AUTHORS

Keldric and Katrina have been married for over 20 years with three children. They both accepted Christ finished work at an early age. They are both graduates of Southern University A&M college in Baton Rouge La. However Keldric completed his undergraduate and graduate work at International Bible Institute in Hacienda Heights, CA.Keldric Emery accepted his call to minister GOD's word and sought further education via St. John Bible Institute (IBI). Keldric and Katrina have taken their personal marriage journey and their years of biblical marriage counseling intertwining them into this helpful book. Please follow them at the following website: http://keministry.com

CONCLUSION

Writing this book over the past year has been a challenge and a joy. We have been challenged in our own marriage while finding joy in knowing that the principles that we have noted are helping us. We called this book "Waging War for your marriage" from the scripture 2 *Corinthians 10:3-4 which says "For though we walk in the flesh, we are not waging war according to the flesh. For the weapons of our warfare are not of the flesh but have divine power to destroy strongholds."* Here Paul admits that we all walk in the flesh because we all are human and deal with some of the same human experiences. Paul also wants to make it clear that although we all experience life the same we shouldn't nor are we required to respond to those life challenges the same way. Paul was saying that we should not respond to life using carnal weapons. The premise of this book is this same notion we cannot fight for our marriages using carnal weapons. We have been married for 20 years and GOD through his word has been teaching us which tools to use. If I don't give prayer and thought to my actions I will use a carnal tool. I will use resentment instead of forgiveness. I will use selfishness instead of considering what is best for our family. I will focus on the wrongs of my spouse rather than focusing on the things that my spouse is doing well. These principles are what created this work.

I think it is important in marriage to remember that the enemy (Satan) hates marriages because it is a reflection of Christ and the church. Solid marriages are effective in changing our community, our children, our generational wealth, our christian witness to the world, our health and so much more. A solid (not perfect) marriage is one of GOD's most effective tools that GOD uses to draw people to himself. It causes others to wonder "how do you make it work"? It is clearly not us but the Spirit of GOD living in us causing us to love one another, to forgive one another, to serve one another as Jesus has done for us through his work on the Cross.

Be encouraged today that your marriage is a tool that GOD is using. Don't give up on your marriage or your spouse. The years you have spent together are worth it. The sacrifices you have made together are important and there is a reward for your waging war. Consider your children, other people who are encouraged by the way you are walking out your life. GOD is pleased by the example that you are portraying.

In the introduction I mentioned two couples that inspired the writing of this book. I am happy to say that the long standing couple has decided to work things out and is in a much better place.

I believe in prayer, and I believe GOD is waiting for someone to stand in the gap for others that are going through hard times. It is also my prayer that if/when we go through hard times there is someone somewhere standing in the gap for us in prayer.

As far as the newly married couple, we plan to give this book to them as a practical guide. We feel it is the least that we can do as they are the first couple that we married.

In closing, consider this last thought. We purchased our current home over 15 years ago. When we initially viewed the home, we were amazed at the beauty and functionality of the house. The appliances, the landscaping, and the layout of the house. What we later found is that the previous home owner staged the house perfectly to hide all the flaws and major work that was needed just to inhabit the home. There were so many problems it took us years to even find them all. From a non functioning hvac system, rooms with no insulation in the attic, broken hot water heater, and roof leakage. It has taken us the better part of 15 years to work on the home to make it feel and look like what we imagined 15 years ago. I use this example to say that marriage is like that old house. It starts with all the glitz and glamor, bells and whistles that one could imagine. Just like our home it is filled with visible and hidden challenges. Marriage takes work and time. You noticed that we titled the book Waging War for your Marriage. You will never completely be done. There will always be areas that you will need to fight to protect your marriage. Just like our home requires constant maintenance and evaluation, so does your marriage. Don't give up on your marriage!! The rewards far outweigh the current challenges that you are experiencing. Fight on and continue to "WAGE WAR for your Marriage".